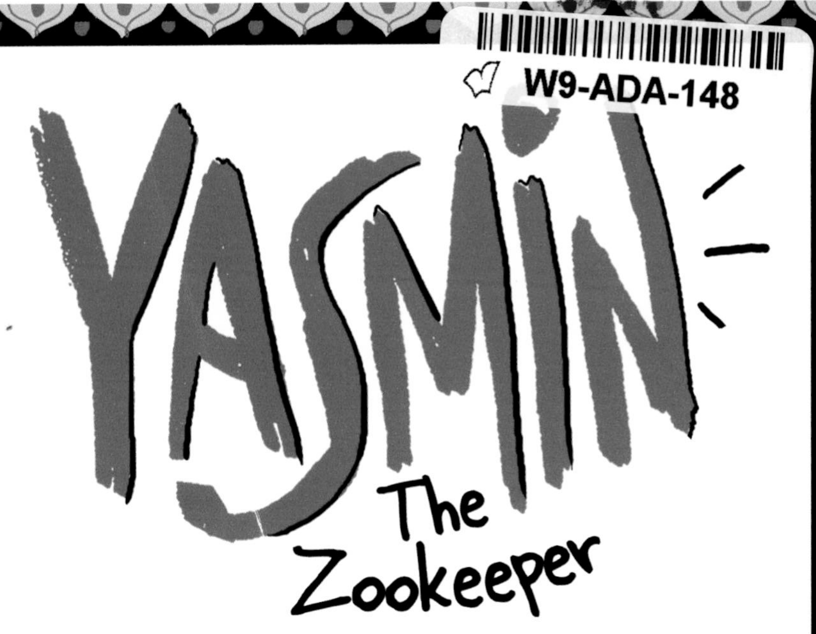

written by
SAADIA FARUQI

illustrated by
HATEM ALY

PICTURE WINDOW BOOKS
a capstone imprint

To Mariam for inspiring me, and Mubashir for helping me find the right words—S.F.

To my sister, Eman, and her amazing girls, Jana and Kenzi—H.A.

Yasmin is published by Picture Window Books, a Capstone imprint
1710 Roe Crest Drive
North Mankato, Minnesota 56003
www.mycapstone.com

Library of Congress Cataloging-in-Publication Data
Names: Faruqi, Saadia, author. | Aly, Hatem, illustrator.
Title: Yasmin the zookeeper / by Saadia Faruqi ; illustrated by Hatem Aly.
Description: North Mankato, Minnesota : Picture Window Books, [2019] | Series: Yasmin | Summary: Yasmin's class is going on a field trip to the zoo, and Yasmin is thrilled when she is chosen to help feed the monkeys; but when she trips and spills their food both she and the monkeys are upset—until she remembers that she has fruit in her lunch bag to share with her new "friends."
Identifiers: LCCN 2018046797| ISBN 9781515837855 (hardcover) | ISBN 9781515845812 (paperback) | ISBN 9781515837909 (eBook PDF)
Subjects: LCSH: Muslim girls—Juvenile fiction. | Pakistani Americans—Juvenile fiction. | School field trips—Juvenile fiction. | Zoos—Juvenile fiction. | Monkeys—Juvenile fiction. | CYAC: Muslims—United States—Fiction. | Pakistani Americans—Fiction. | School field trips—Fiction. | Zoos—Fiction.
Classification: LCC PZ7.1.F373 Yo 2019 | DDC [E]—dc23
LC record available at https://lccn.loc.gov/2018046797

Editor: Kristen Mohn
Designer: Lori Bye

Design Elements:
Shutterstock: Art and Fashion, rangsan paidaen

Printed in the United States of America.
PA49

TABLE OF CONTENTS

CHAPTER 1

Field Trip

Yasmin and Mama walked together to school one morning. At least Mama walked. Yasmin skipped. She was very excited. Today her class was taking a field trip to the zoo.

"Here's your lunch, Yasmin," said Mama, handing her a brown bag. "There's fruit in there for a snack too."

Yasmin hugged her mother and boarded the bright yellow bus.

Yasmin looked around. She'd never been on a school bus before.

Emma waved to her. "Yasmin, sit with me!"

"Hey, your brown bag is just like mine!" Yasmin said.

"Mine too!" Ali said, popping up behind them. His bag was big! The girls laughed.

"Ready, class?" asked Ms. Alex.

"Ready!" the students shouted.

The ride to the zoo was very long. The students sang songs and told jokes. Ali's jokes were the funniest.

"What's a kangaroo's favorite game?" he asked. "Hop Scotch!"

CHAPTER 2

Meet the Animals

The zoo was full of all kinds of animals. Ms. Alex led the way. First was a pool for seals.

"Look, they're taking a bath!" Yasmin said.

A seal swam toward them. It splashed them all with water!

"Don't stand too close," Ms. Alex warned. "Remember, this is the animals' home, not yours."

Next they walked to the elephant yard. Yasmin counted three elephants: a mama, a baba, and a baby.

"How adorable!" cried Emma.

The baba elephant walked over and snatched Ali's cap from his head.

"Hey!" shouted Ali. "Give it back!"

Finally, they reached the monkey area. *Bandars!* Yasmin's favorite.

A zookeeper was waiting for them. "Hello, kids," he said. "I'm Dave. It's the monkeys' lunchtime. Would anyone like to help me?"

All the students raised their hands. Yasmin tried to raise hers the highest.

"Please pick me," she whispered.

"How about you, in the purple top?" Dave said. He pointed to Yasmin.

"Yes!" Yasmin cheered.

Dave gave Yasmin a big bowl of fruit. It had slices of apples, bananas, and oranges.

"Fruit salad!" said Emma.

Yasmin carefully walked toward the monkeys. They squealed and chattered with excitement.

But suddenly, Yasmin tripped!

The bowl of fruit went flying . . .

right into the pond.

CHAPTER 3

Hungry Monkeys

The monkeys were upset. They wanted their lunch! They screeched and howled. Yasmin's heart thumped. Would Dave be angry too?

Then she remembered the lunch bag in her backpack.

What had Mama packed?

Yasmin opened it.

A banana!

"Can I share my fruit with the monkeys?" Yasmin asked Dave.

“I guess it would be all right, just this once,” Dave said. He broke the banana into pieces for Yasmin.

A baby monkey climbed onto Yasmin’s lap. She held very still as the monkey nibbled banana from her hand. It tickled!

Then Emma took out her brown bag. “I have two oranges,” she offered.

The other students took out their brown bags too. Soon all the monkeys had fruit to eat.

Yasmin

"Now it's time for *our* lunch!" Ms. Alex said. "Let's go to the playground and eat."

Yasmin waved goodbye to the monkeys.

"Bye, bandars! I'll come again someday, little friends!"

Think About It, Talk About It

- Yasmin is a little nervous about riding a school bus for the first time. How does Emma make Yasmin feel more comfortable? How would you help a friend who felt nervous or scared?

- When Yasmin drops the fruit, she has to think fast to come up with a solution to her problem. Think about a time in your life when something went wrong. What did you do?

- Imagine you are going to a zoo that has every animal in the world. If you could only choose three animals to visit, which three would you choose? Why?

Learn Urdu with Yasmin!

Yasmin's family speaks both English and Urdu. Urdu is a language from Pakistan. Maybe you already know some Urdu words!

baba (BAH-bah)—father

bandar (BAHN-dar)—monkey

hijab (HEE-jahb)—scarf covering the hair

jaan (jahn)—life; a sweet nickname for a loved one

kameez (kuh-MEEZ)—long tunic or shirt

mama (MAH-mah)—mother

naan (nahn)—flatbread baked in the oven

nana (NAH-nah)—grandfather on mother's side

nani (NAH-nee)—grandmother on mother's side

salaam (sah-LAHM)—hello

Pakistan Fun Facts

Yasmin and her family are proud of their Pakistani culture. Yasmin loves to share facts about Pakistan!

Location

Pakistan is on the continent of Asia, with India on one side and Afghanistan on the other.

Islamabad
PAKISTAN

Population

Pakistan's population is about 207,774,520, making it the world's sixth-most populous country.

National Bird

Pakistan's national bird is the chukar, a game bird from the pheasant family.

Zoo

Lahore Zoo in Punjab, Pakistan, is one of the largest zoos in South Asia.

Make a Bendy Monkey!

SUPPLIES:

- construction paper
- scissors
- crayons or markers
- small googly eyes
- glue
- brown and yellow pipe cleaners

STEPS:

1. Cut an oval and a circle from the construction paper to make the monkey's body and head.

2. Glue googly eyes onto the head and draw the rest of the monkey's face. Glue the head to the body.

3. Glue brown pipe cleaners to the back of the body to make the arms and legs. Use another to make the tail. Make a curl at the tip!

4. To give the monkey a banana, cut and bend a small piece of a yellow pipe cleaner and place it in the monkey's hand.

5. After the glue dries, bend the arms, legs, and tail into any pose you'd like. Wrap your bendy monkey around a pencil to make a pencil pal!

About the Author

Saadia Faruqi is a Pakistani American writer, interfaith activist, and cultural sensitivity trainer previously profiled in *O Magazine*. She is author of the adult short story collection, *Brick Walls: Tales of Hope & Courage from Pakistan*. Her essays have been published in *Huffington Post*, *Upworthy*, and *NBC Asian America*. She resides in Houston, Texas, with her husband and children.

About the Illustrator

Hatem Aly is an Egyptian-born illustrator whose work has been featured in multiple publications worldwide. He currently lives in beautiful New Brunswick, Canada, with his wife, son, and more pets than people. When he is not dipping cookies in a cup of tea or staring at blank pieces of paper, he is usually drawing books. One of the books he illustrated is *The Inquisitor's Tale* by Adam Gidwitz, which won a Newbery Honor and other awards, despite Hatem's drawings of a farting dragon, a two-headed cat, and stinky cheese.